# CUMBRIA LIBRARIES

KT-491-494

Libraries, books and more..........

Please return/renew this item by the last date shown.
Library items may also be renewed by phone on
030 33 33 1234 (24hours) or via our website

www.cumbria.gov.uk/libraries

**Cumbria Libraries**

# CLIC
**Interactive Catalogue**

Ask for a CLIC password

For Rosie
Who decided to learn the flute. Phew.
Dad x

A TEMPLAR BOOK
First published in the UK in 2019 by Templar Books,
an imprint of Bonnier Books UK,
The Plaza, 535 King's Road, London, SW10 0SZ

www.templarco.co.uk
www.bonnierbooks.co.uk

ISBN 978-1-78741-513-3
EBook ISBN: 978-1-78741-619-2

Edited by Katie Haworth
Designed by Marty Cleary
Production by Neil Randles

FSC
www.fsc.org

MIX
Paper from
responsible sources
FSC® C023114

Printed in the United Kingdom

# The JOLLEY-ROGERS and the PIRATE PIPER

## JONNY DUDDLE

templar
books

# PROLOGUE

A thick fog covered Dull-on-Sea, lazily
rolling off the moonless ocean.
    One nautical mile from shore, a bowsprit
split the gloom, dragging tattered sails and
a battered hull behind it. The deck
of the ship seemed alive
and quivered as though
it had been lined
with fur.

At the helm, Captain Horatio Rattus eyed the compass. One hand gripped the wheel, while the other lifted a brass flute from its case.

Not long now, my beauties! I'll be turnin' her hard to starboard, so ye should all be preparin' to swim!

In Dull-on-Sea, Arthur Poppycock had dozed off at his desk in the harbour office. He had changed jobs recently; he'd been far too scared to return as security guard at Dull-on-Sea Museum after it had been raided by ghost pirates.

The best thing about his new job, as the night-shift harbour master, was that nobody

arrived by sea once darkness fell. Arthur did point out that the thieving ghost pirates had arrived in the early hours of the morning, but everyone assured him that he would never see a ghost pirate again.

Every night, Arthur would finish his crossword and a small glass of rum and let the gentle lapping of the waves against the harbour wall soothe him to sleep. The seagulls would wake him at sunrise, before anyone noticed he'd slept.

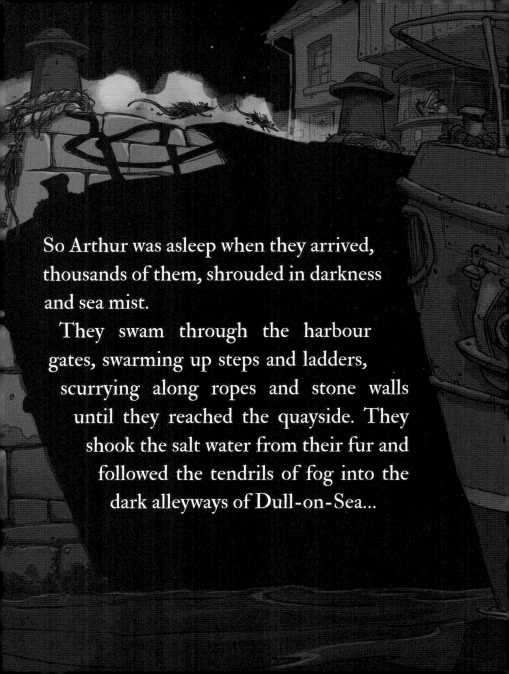

So Arthur was asleep when they arrived, thousands of them, shrouded in darkness and sea mist.

They swam through the harbour gates, swarming up steps and ladders, scurrying along ropes and stone walls until they reached the quayside. They shook the salt water from their fur and followed the tendrils of fog into the dark alleyways of Dull-on-Sea...

# 1.
# RATS

In her cottage on Sea View Terrace, Mrs Bumble sat up in bed, cup and saucer in hand. She gazed at the sunlight streaming through the window and supped her tea.

She considered herself very lucky to have such a splendid sea view and liked to spend a few minutes every morning watching the waves crash on the shore. Mrs Bumble was always very busy being a busybody and she enjoyed these moments of peace and calm before the start of another busy day.

But this morning her peace and calm was disturbed by a scratching noise.

It was a loud scratching noise and it seemed to be coming from beneath her floorboards. It was joined by another – this one behind her head, behind her plump pillows, behind her floral wallpaper and deep within her bedroom wall. And there were more scratching noises coming from beneath her open window, where something was scratchily scampering up the climbing rose that clung to her cottage.

A black claw scrabbled along the window ledge, searching for grip, before hoisting up a great, dark lump of fur.

Two red eyes stared at Mrs Bumble and a nose and whiskers twitched.

"RATS!" screamed Mrs Bumble.

**RATS!**

screamed Arthur Poppycock, rudely awakened by an enormous black rat that was noisily munching on the remnants of his double-chocolate muffin.

Arthur peered out the window to see a seagull flapping seaward, escaping the rats that covered the harbour office, the yachts, the fishing boats and the quayside.

# RATS!

screamed Sheila Wobley, Mrs Bumble's neighbour on Sea View Terrace.

She opened the door to her spare bedroom to find rats devouring her washing. The wash basket did smell faintly of fish and chips, so perhaps the rats thought it was food.

Dull-on-Sea was infested with rats. They were everywhere – not only in every house on Sea View Terrace – but all through town.

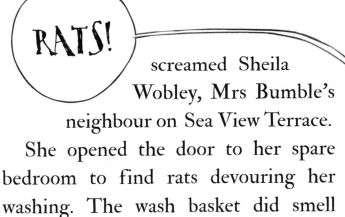

The museum had closed as soon as it had opened, when the curator had spotted rats chewing on dinosaur bones. The library was open, but the librarians were moving all the books to higher shelves because the rats had taken a liking to paper.

Chief Inspector Klewless, of Dull-on-Sea Police had locked himself in a cell because he had a bit of a phobia of rats. He asked to be notified when the council's pest control department had cleared the police station.

Matilda had woken early and staggered downstairs in her pyjamas to see if there was a clean school dress in the laundry basket.

She couldn't quite open her eyes. It was

a Friday morning and almost the end of term, so waking up was getting much more difficult. As Matilda wandered through the kitchen she wondered why her mum was standing on the table with a broom.

The cat flap banged, swinging on its hinges, and Matilda's cat hurtled past.

"Good morning, Fluff," said Matilda with a yawn, but Fluff didn't stop.

In the utility room, Matilda rummaged in the laundry basket and found a clean dress. When she yanked it from beneath the other clothes, a big ball of black fur fell to the floor and scurried beneath the washing machine.

"ANOTHER ONE?" screamed Matilda's dad.

She hadn't noticed until now, but her dad was balancing on a tall cupboard. Matilda suddenly felt much more awake.

"Another what?" she asked.

"RATS!" said Matilda's dad. "RATS! EVERYWHERE!"

Back on Sea View Terrace, Mrs Bumble reached for her phone. She would call the council to see what they would do – she hadn't moved to Sea View Terrace to have rodents spoil her view.

# 2.
# FIDDLE PRACTICE

"What's that 'orrible noise?" screamed Grandpa, his head popping up from a hatch on the fo'c'sle. "It sounds like a kraken pullin' the gizzards from a mermaid!"

"Pardon?" said Jim Lad, moving one headphone aside. He'd been listening to some very loud heavy metal music

to drown out Nugget's fiddle practice.

Nugget had just started learning the fiddle, which is very like a violin, but of a type favoured by pirates and rogues. Grandpa had played his fiddle across the oceans and seas, until recently passing it on to Nugget.

Many years ago, he had been given his fiddle by a mysterious sea hag and seemed to recall his music had not been popular with other pirates. He did attract crowds of landlubbing children whenever he played ashore, but – other than Nugget and Jim – he had never been keen on sproglets.

Unfortunately, Grandpa had been forced to give up playing when the King chopped off his hand and he had stashed his fiddle in an old sea chest – but that's a story for another time. Right now he was regretting that he had given it to Nugget.

"Curses!" hollered Grandpa. "Why didn't I palm her off with my flute?"

But Grandpa knew why he'd given Nugget his fiddle. She'd been obsessed with it since she was a baby. She would rock wide-eyed in her cot as Grandpa skipped about her cabin, playing sea shanties on it and singing in his croaky voice.

On her fourth birthday, Grandpa gifted the fiddle to Nugget and started to

teach her how to play. He told Nugget
that the more she practised, the better she
would get. That was a few weeks ago, but
her playing hadn't much improved.

It wasn't because Nugget was short
on enthusiasm – she loved playing
her fiddle and practised several
times each day. Whenever
the Jolley-Rogers spotted her
opening her fiddle case they
would all find something to do,
as far away as possible.

Jim Lad found that this
was the best time to don his
headphones.

Jim's dad usually resorted to ship maintenance and had finally got around to tarring the deadeyes. He was listening to country and western on the ancient personal stereo he'd had since he was a boy. His headphones weren't as good as Jim's but he was also further away from Nugget and hanging over the side of the ship, caked in tar. Bones, the Jolley-Rogers' three-legged dog, was howling on the poop deck.

Jim's mum was relaxing in the crow's nest, high up the main mast, where the screeches of Nugget's strings were whisked away on the wind. She was eye-splicing a rope and listening to Dull FM:

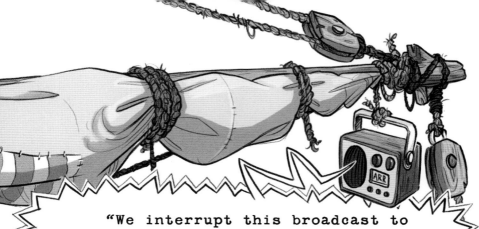

"We interrupt this broadcast to bring news from Dull-on-Sea, which is battling a sudden rat infestation. The mayor has called an emergency meeting of the town council and would ask that anyone with relevant experience of pest control should attend."

Jim's mum finished the splice, hoisted herself over the rail of the crow's nest and slid down to speak to Jim on the deck below. She nudged a headphone to one side and whispered in his ear.

"Fancy a trip to Dull-on-Sea, Jim?"

# 3.
# AN AUDIENCE

"Ahoy, Matilda!" Jim Lad yelled from the prow of the Jolley-Rogers' amphibious truck.

A few hours earlier, Jim had sent Squawk, the Jolley-Rogers' macaw,

to visit Matilda with news of their imminent arrival. Matilda was waiting on the beach as the truck chug-chug-chugged its way through the surf and onto the sand, shedding seaweed, salt water and shellfish. Jim's mum had decided it would be a good idea to anchor the *Blackhole* offshore because she didn't want Dull-on-Sea's rats coming aboard.

Jim jumped off the truck as it came to a halt and gave Matilda the biggest pirate hug he could muster before they both ran off across the beach giggling and weaving between the few tourists that were left in Dull-on-Sea.

The rats didn't seem to like the beach,

so a few locals were taking refuge there too, enjoying the warm but slightly overcast weather. Bones chased after Jim and Matilda, barking excitedly, his wooden leg leaving a trail of evenly spaced hollows in the sand.

Nugget hoisted herself out of her car seat and climbed onto the bonnet of the truck. She swung her fiddle to her shoulder, held her bow aloft and started to play.

Matilda stopped dead. "Is that Nugget?"

"Yeh," said Jim. "It's 'orrible! I have to put my 'eadphones on to drown it out!"

"It's BEAUTIFUL!" said Matilda. "Let's go and listen!"

Jim, confused, took a moment to fully

understand what Matilda had said.

But before he could answer, Matilda was gone, running across the beach towards Nugget. By the time Jim caught up with her beside the truck, Nugget had an audience, mostly

made up of gawping, swaying children.

Jim's mum and dad looked just as confused as him, and Jim's dad had already stuffed his ears with corks.

"Would it be okay if I record you playing?" Matilda asked when Nugget paused to scratch her nose.

Nugget looked chuffed; finally someone appreciated her music! The rest of the Jolley-Rogers looked aghast.

"Aye!" said Nugget with an enormous grin. "That'd be just fine!"

Matilda's mum had recently given her an old phone, and Matilda took it everywhere. It was just the thing for recording Nugget's music. Nugget played the three songs that Grandpa Rogers had been teaching her with renewed gusto. They weren't perfect, but Matilda and the other children were entranced.

When Nugget finished (and she only stopped because she had run out of tunes) all the children were a little dazed. They looked at one another, overcome by what they had heard. Then there was a smattering of applause and they all wandered back towards their parents, frisbees and sandcastles.

"That was brilliant!" said Matilda. "I could listen to your music all day long! I'm going to play it tonight to help me get to sleep. It's so beautiful and soothing..."

"Are you okay, Matilda?" asked Jim. Nugget slammed him on the head with her fiddle.

"I'm fine," said Matilda. "But I think we'd better hurry if we're going to make the meeting at the Town Hall!"

# 1.
# EMERGENCY MEETING

Harvey Carrot, Mayor of Dull-on-Sea, had called an emergency meeting. All the councillors were there and the Town Hall was packed with townsfolk. Norbert Grimes, senior rat catcher for the council's pest control department, had spent all morning trying to rid the building of rats.
He had a large, wriggling sack

slung over his shoulder and was prowling the perimeter of the hall with a net, peering into corners and under benches.

Jim Lad had tagged along with Matilda and was sitting near the back of the hall with her parents. He had promised to report back to the rest of the Jolley-Rogers. Matilda could see her neighbours, Mrs Bevan from eighty-seven and Mr Shaw from thirty-four, along with plenty of school friends sitting alongside their parents. She smiled and waved to Ruby, the girl she sat next to in class.

"People of Dull-on-Sea," the mayor began, "thank you for attending this emergency meeting. You may have noticed that we have a bit of a problem with rats."

"They chewed holes in my washing!" shouted Sheila Wobley.

"The blighters stole my sandwiches!" added Mr Shaw, who had taken his wife for a disastrous rat-infested picnic the previous day.

"They've nibbled the corners of all our bottom shelf books!" wailed Bunty Bookish, the librarian.

"Yes, yes, we know the rats are causing no end of problems," grumbled the mayor. "Our very reliable pest control expert, Mr Grimes, has been working flat out, but he has never seen an infestation like this. For every rat he catches, another two appear!"

At the back of the hall, bent double and swinging his net beneath a bench, Norbert Grimes scowled. He came from a long line of rat-catchers. The Grimes family had been proud rat-catchers for centuries. He had never been defeated by rats before.

"I pay my tax!" shouted Mrs Bevan, who liked to regularly write letters of complaint to the council. "I expect Dull-on-Sea to be pest free!"

"Me too!" shouted Mrs Bumble.

"Sort it out!" grumbled Mr Shaw.

"ORDER! ORDER!" hollered the

mayor, ruffled by the unrest in the hall. "I know you are all very, very unhappy, but what should we do?"

As the townsfolk sat in silence, scratching their heads, Matilda heard the click-clack of footsteps approaching. They stopped outside the doors and there was a pause.

Everyone stopped scratching their heads and turned to look.

"Erm, please enter..." said the mayor.

The doors swung open to reveal a raggedy figure, wearing a tattered tailcoat, an unfeasibly tall top hat and long pointed shoes. In his hand he held a flute.

"Captain Horatio Rattus," he said, with a bow. "The Pirate Piper. At your service."

He put the flute to his thin, blue lips and played a few bars of soft melodious music. Rats appeared at his feet, running in circles around him, squeaking excitedly.

Beyond his hooked, wart-encrusted nose, in the dark shadows beneath the dusty brim of his top hat, his eyes smiled. He had them all hooked. Not just the swarming rats, that were bewitched by his flute, but also the mayor, the townsfolk and particularly the children.

Even rat-catcher Norbert Grimes was looking reluctantly impressed.

"I can solve your rat problem," the Pirate Piper declared. "And I will do it for a modest price."

"Splendid!" said the the mayor. "When you say a 'modest price', what are you thinking?"

"Oh, I don't know..." slurred the Pirate Piper, staring intently at the mayor. "How does ten thousand pounds sound? In notes or gold, I'm really not a fussy man..."

"TEN THOUSAND POUNDS?" The mayor spluttered. "Are you MAD?"

"Very well," said the Pirate Piper, slowly making to leave. The rats left his heels and spread themselves about the hall. "I will let you sort this problem out for yourselves…"

"WAIT!" screamed Mrs Bumble, arms outstretched towards the fiddler, but head twisted to face the mayor. "You can't let him leave! WHAT ABOUT THE RATS?"

Mrs Bumble's voice was joined by other protests. Everyone wanted the Pirate Piper to stay.

"Yes, yes! Very well!" Mayor Carrot grumbled, wary of upsetting the Dull-on-Sea electorate. "We will give this… erm… gentleman… a chance."

# 5.
# THE PIPER

A crowd had gathered outside the Town Hall, spilling from its doors to witness the Pirate Piper deliver on his promise.

At its centre was Captain Horatio Rattus, flute in hand. He held the flute to his lips, waiting a few moments to add to the drama and suspense.

The crowd was silent, barely breathing, as he began to play.

The soft notes that left the flute floated on the morning breeze, spreading through the town. Almost immediately came the scratching and squeaking of a thousand rats, scurrying through alleyways and sewers, over rooftops and gardens, bursting from drains and bins and shops and houses. They swarmed towards the Pirate Piper.

The crowd gasped and held onto each other as the rats ran towards them, but the Piper skipped across the town square and disappeared from view with the

rats thronging behind him, as thousands more joined the furry congregation.

The crowd remained silent, listening to the flute in the distance as it travelled street by street through Dull-on-Sea.

They heard it travel up the hill, through the new estates, along the clifftops on the edge of town, down the funicular railway, where they caught a glimpse of the Piper on the roof of a slope car, encircled by thousands of dancing rats.

Then the music grew louder again as the Pirate Piper returned to the centre of town. He led the rats down the high street and across the promenade and into the harbour, where the quayside was awash

with fur and the pattering of claws.

An hour earlier, Captain Horatio Rattus had arrived unheard, while almost every resident of Dull-on-Sea was at the emergency meeting. His hulking ship, the *Black Death*, with its patched sails, frayed ropes and flaking paint, looked down-at-heel when moored beside the sparkling yachts and fishing boats in the harbour. It cast dark shadows across their varnished decks.

Now the Pirate Piper skipped along the rail of his ship, merrily dancing and playing his flute, while the rats watched and listened, mesmerised.

Three gangplanks creaked as thousands of rats scurried aboard, following wooden walkways into three enormous crates, which were waiting on deck.

When the last of the rats had entered the crates to join the writhing, wriggling mass of fur and tails, the Pirate Piper unsheathed a knife from his belt and severed a rope. Block and tackle rattled and squealed as ropes spun, pulling the hatches on each crate closed before hoisting them high into the air. The rats were trapped, suspended in the *Black Death's* rigging.

The growing crowd, many of whom had followed the Pirate Piper and the rats at a safe distance, clapped and cheered and the Piper could not resist a bow, doffing his hat with a flourish.

"Behold, good folk of Dull-on-Sea!" he boomed. "I, Captain Horatio Rattus, am true to my word and them scurvy rats have been proper contained!"

"I shall be taking 'em out to sea and castin' 'em into the deepest depths!" He continued. "Ye shall no longer be sufferin' the ravages of them rats! Ye shall be free from their fleas and disease. I ask only for my payment in return!"

There was another cheer and a polite

round of applause. As the *Black Death* sailed slowly out of the harbour, Mrs Bumble wiped a tear of joy from her eye with a tissue.

She may have been less joyful if she had seen the Pirate Piper break his promise to throw the rats in the sea. Once he was a safe distance from shore, he carefully lowered the three rat-filled crates into the hold of his ship.

# 6.

# PAYMENT

Captain Horatio Rattus marched into the council offices with a swagger, head held high. He rested his flute over one shoulder, while a flea-bitten rat sat on the other.

"I'm here to see Mayor Carrot," he declared, and walked straight past the receptionist and up a grand staircase to the mayor's office. Harvey Carrot had his back to the door, and was lounging in a

sturdy leather chair admiring the view of Dull-on-Sea. The Pirate Piper let himself in and marched to the mayor's desk, tapping on its green leather surface with his flute. Mayor Carrot turned around slowly and, disgruntled, leant on his elbows with his fists clenched firmly together.

"Well, look who we have here!" he said. "Would you like to walk back outside and knock? Or should I call security and..."

"My job is done!" the Pirate Piper interrupted. "That will be ten thousand pounds Mr Mayor. Ye'll pay me in gold, silver or twenty-pound notes, whichever ye'll be findin' easier."

"Well, here's the thing," said Harvey

Carrot. "When I'm not playing mayor, I'm a bit of a businessman, and I don't think you've earned ten thousand pounds. I'm happy to write you a cheque for one."

"One what?" scowled Captain Rattus. "And I won't be acceptin' yer cheques."

"One thousand pounds," replied the mayor. "I think that's a fair price. What do you say? If you want it in cash, you'll have to wait until tomorrow."

"I named me price, you squab," said Rattus firmly. "And I think ye'll be findin' that was TEN thousand pounds. I took yer scurvy rats and now I want me gold!"

"Ah, but we had no contract, no handshake. People were emotional," said the mayor. "Now I've had time to reflect, I think the price was too high. It was only a few rats, after all. Our chap in the council, Norbert Grimes, would've sorted it all out eventually. One thousand pounds. You can take it or leave it."

"Refuse to pay! I dare ye..." growled the Pirate Piper.

"Oh, okay," said the mayor, chuckling and rubbing his enormous hairy palms together. "I refuse."

The Pirate Piper turned on his heels and left, muttering under his breath. Mayor Carrot was rather pleased with himself. He spun around in his chair to get back to enjoying the view, but was greeted by a great, black, flea-bitten rat, squatting on the window ledge and giving him the evils.

# 7.

# SLEEPWALKING

It was the dead of night. Nothing stirred in Dull-on-Sea. Matilda had fallen asleep listening to her recording of Nugget's flute, which played on a loop from the phone at her bedside.

Arthur Poppycock had fallen asleep too, after polishing off a large glass of rum and a jam doughnut. He had barely slept when the rats were infesting the harbour, but since the Pirate Piper had weaved his magic throughout the town, he felt much more relaxed. He liked Dull-on-Sea to be rat free, and now there were probably fewer rats in Dull-on-Sea than there had ever been.

So Arthur didn't see the shabby old ship return to the harbour. He didn't see the shadowy figure emerge from its deck, his threadbare tailcoat flapping behind him. And he didn't see the same figure raise a flute to his lips, or hear the tunes that slipped from that flute, drifting on the sea breeze, worming their way into children's bedrooms all over town.

When the soft melodies of the flute reached their ears, the

children sat up in their beds. They put on their dressing gowns and slippers and ambled out of their rooms. But they weren't awake. They were bewitched by the Pirate Piper's music.

The flute controlled them, drew them to the centre of town, across gardens and flowerbeds. Bathed in the orange light of street lamps, they passed locked-up shops and sleepwalked through deserted parks.

But Matilda hadn't budged. She was fast asleep in her own bed, serenaded by the screeches of Nugget's fiddle.

The Pirate Piper was playing his flute on the bandstand by the seafront. He had been there for almost an hour and was now surrounded by hundreds of children with mucky feet or mud-stained slippers. Nobody had arrived for quite some time

weaving down the cliff face and onto the wind-swept beach.

But the Piper hadn't noticed a dark, feline shape blending with the shadows, skipping silently between the pools of darkness and watching his every move.

# 8.
# THE DISAPPEARED

Matilda was woken by her cat, standing on her chest and pawing at the duvet. Her phone was still playing Nugget's music.

"What's up, Fluff?" asked Matilda.

Fluff jumped from the bed, across the floor and onto the window ledge, where she paced back and forth rubbing her sides against the glass and miaowing loudly.

Matilda rubbed her eyes and rolled out of bed, joining Fluff at the window. Outside, she could could see huddles of people, chattering and pointing and talking on their mobile phones. Matilda thought it was a bit strange to see so many grown-ups on the street in their dressing gowns and night clothes. A police car whizzed past, blue lights flashing and sirens blaring.

She walked downstairs, closely followed by Fluff, and found her mum and dad eating breakfast, whispering anxiously.

"Oh, good morning, Matilda!" said her mum, with an unconvincing smile.

"Would you like some toast?"

"Have we got Pirate Pops...?" asked Matilda, wearily pulling a chair out from the table. "What's with the worried faces? And the police cars?"

"Some children have disappeared," said her mum, looking very concerned. "As soon as we heard, we came to check on

you and were so happy to find you safely tucked up in bed."

"Mind you, I'm not sure how you could sleep with that horrible screeching on your phone," added her dad, trying to change the subject. Feeling flustered, he missed Matilda's bowl completely and poured a pile of Pirate Pops onto the table. "Oh... Um... But your mother told me to leave it on. She said you liked it and it helped you get to sleep. You kids listen to some rubbish nowadays. I can lend you some proper music if you like. I know quite a lot about high fidelity music, y'know."

"So who's missing? Which children?" asked Matilda, ignoring her dad and very worried about Ruby and her other friends.

"Well... We had the radio on earlier, and it's... erm... All of them," her mum replied. "All of the children are missing!"

Nobody said much after that. They finished their breakfast and Matilda got ready for school. While she waited for her mum to dry her hair, she had to endure a demonstration of her dad's 'high-fidelity music' in the lounge.

"It's almost like being there!" he beamed, playing a jumble of jazz at high volume. "When I close my eyes I'm transported to the 1950s, in a smoky New York bar, full of cool cats. What do you think, Tilda?"

"It's not so bad, I suppose," Matilda mumbled. "Could you play Nugget's music? From my phone?"

"That screechy racket? On my stereo equipment?" said her dad.

"Please?" Matilda held out her phone.

Moments later, it was playing through her dad's speakers, and Nugget's music filled the house. Matilda noticed a rat run up to the patio window and try to claw its way in, which she thought was a bit strange.

Then her mum appeared downstairs and it was time to go.

# 9.
# SCHOOL

On the walk to town with her mum, Matilda felt very uncomfortable. Everyone they passed stared at her, curtains twitched and shopkeepers peered from empty shops. A police car stopped across the road and the two officers inside watched them walk by, open mouthed, before grabbing their radios.

As they passed the Town Hall, they noticed Mrs Bevan with a placard.

"I heard that Mayor Carrot refused to pay the Piper," said Mrs Bevan, who had decided a protest was in order, even though she didn't have children of her own. "After the pub, Mervyn Wobley fell asleep on a bench on the seafront. He said he woke up to some funny music and dropped his chips."

Once Mrs Bevan had updated Matilda's mum on everything that had happened, they carried on to school. On most mornings the front of the school was a riot of children, parents and badly parked cars. But today it was deserted.

"See you later," said Matilda's mum, kissing Matilda on the forehead. "Wait for me to pick you up. See you at three!"

Matilda was only at school for an hour. The teacher said she wouldn't want the other children to miss out on important lessons, before she ran to the staffroom crying. So, Matilda stared out of the window, waiting for her mum to get out of work and collect her. Occasionally a police car would fly along the road.

The classroom felt very empty.

On a normal school day there would be mayhem if their teacher ran off crying to the staffroom and left her pupils unsupervised. Even Matilda's desk felt

empty, and lonely without Ruby sitting next to her.

"Why am I the only one...?" Matilda wondered. "Why didn't I disappear too? Why did Mrs Bevan think it had something to do with the Piper?"

After almost an hour of wondering, Matilda's mum turned up.

As the sun rose higher over the troubled town, the Jolley-Rogers sailed their ship into Dull-on-Sea. Jim's mum was happy to moor the *Blackhole* in the harbour now

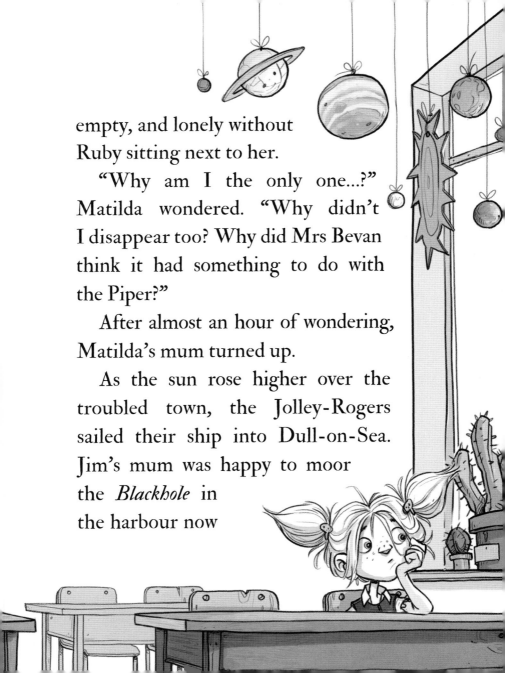

the rats had disappeared. While Jim and his dad secured the gangplank, Arthur Poppycock donned his harbour master's hat and marched across the quayside to greet them.

"You might want to keep your nippers onboard!" said Arthur, pointing to Jim. "All the children went missing last night! Every child in Dull-on-Sea! Gone! Just like that! I didn't see or hear a thing!"

"Dad!" said Jim, urgently. "I've gotta go to Tilda's house!"

"There's not much point," said Arthur Poppycock. "They're all gone. The police are on it though. I'm sure they'll have all the children home by the end of the day. Mind you, Chief Inspector Klewless was on the radio earlier saying he was a bit baffled."

"Aye, lad," said Jim's dad, putting a hand on his shoulder. "Probably best stayin' here, safe on the ship, 'til we know what's goin' on..."

# 10.
# THE CAVE

As soon as Matilda arrived home, Fluff started walking figures of eight around her ankles, miaowing, purring and wrapping her tail around Matilda's legs. The cat ran across to the patio door, and mewed loudly until Matilda opened it.

But Fluff didn't disappear across the garden as she normally would, she darted back and forth, in and out of the door, miaowing and glaring at Matilda.

"Fancy a snack, Tilda?" called her mum,

who was now in the kitchen.

"You get comfy on the sofa and I'll bring you a hot chocolate and some biscuits."

But Matilda was already following Fluff through the patio door into the garden. She pulled her bike out of the shed, fastened her helmet and watched Fluff disappear through the back gate.

She pedalled furiously to catch up, but Fluff was running at quite a pace towards the harbour.

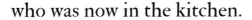

A few minutes later, she found Fluff sitting beside the *Blackhole*, miaowing as loudly as she could. Bones' head popped over the ship's rail, followed by a furiously wagging tail. He bounded down the gangplank and gave Fluff's head a great, slobbery lick. She reciprocated by pushing her cheeks firmly against Bones' face, pacing back and forth and purring in delight.

"I see our pets are reunited!" Jim chuckled, hanging

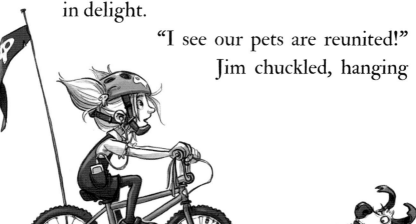

from the rigging above. "I'm mighty relieved, Matilda! I'd been told yer was one of them 'disappeared' kids..."

"Nah, I didn't disappear," said Matilda. "But all the other children have gone. I'm wondering if Fluff knows something we don't."

Jim grabbed a rope and

swung down to join them.

As soon as he landed on the cobbles, Fluff ran off again, this time along the seafront, with Bones hurtling after her.

"Jump aboard, Jim!" said Matilda. "I'll give you a backy!"

Jim climbed astride Matilda's back wheel, wrapped one arm around her waist, and they rushed after their pets. Fluff and Bones had quite a head start, but luckily Jim had his telescope and managed to keep them in view. With Dull-on-Sea's rat infestation, most of the tourists had gone home, so it wasn't too hard to follow a cat and a dog along the promenade, past the pier, across the bandstand and onto

the coast road out of town.

They crossed the headland at the end of the beach, Matilda huffing and puffing as she peddled uphill with Jim weighing down her back wheel, but that made the downhill on the other side so much more fun.

But just as they were enjoying the wind in their hair, the effortless acceleration and the slightly uncontrolled speed wobbles, Matilda slammed on her brakes and skidded to a stop.

Fluff was sitting atop a signpost that pointed towards some rickety steps on the side of the cliff, while Bones was sniffing the sea air, searching for a scent. Jim, who had been thrown over Matilda's shoulders and the handlebars by the sudden stop, was lying in a heap on the road.

"I think they want us to go down there," he groaned.

The beach was deserted. The wind was picking up, with dark clouds gathering out to sea. Waves crashed, dragging pebbles, shells and driftwood back and forth onto the shore, but there was no sign of the missing children. Jim was looking through his telescope, scanning the length of the beach.

Fluff had remained at the top of the steps on the signpost – she wasn't a fan of blustery beaches – but Bones was darting

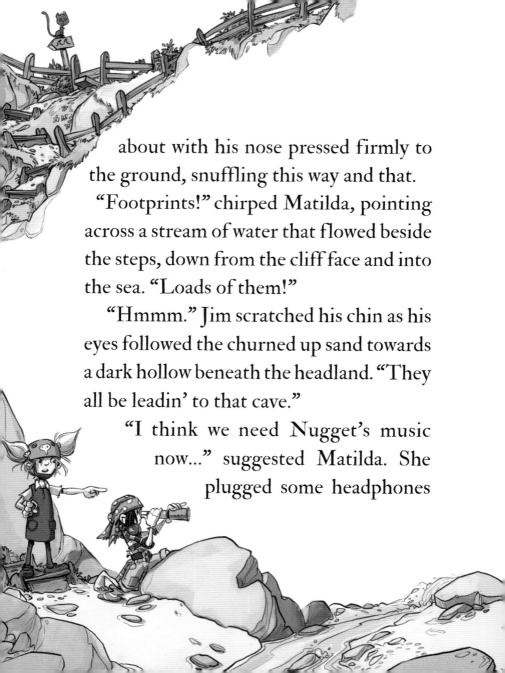

about with his nose pressed firmly to the ground, snuffling this way and that.

"Footprints!" chirped Matilda, pointing across a stream of water that flowed beside the steps, down from the cliff face and into the sea. "Loads of them!"

"Hmmm." Jim scratched his chin as his eyes followed the churned up sand towards a dark hollow beneath the headland. "They all be leadin' to that cave."

"I think we need Nugget's music now..." suggested Matilda. She plugged some headphones

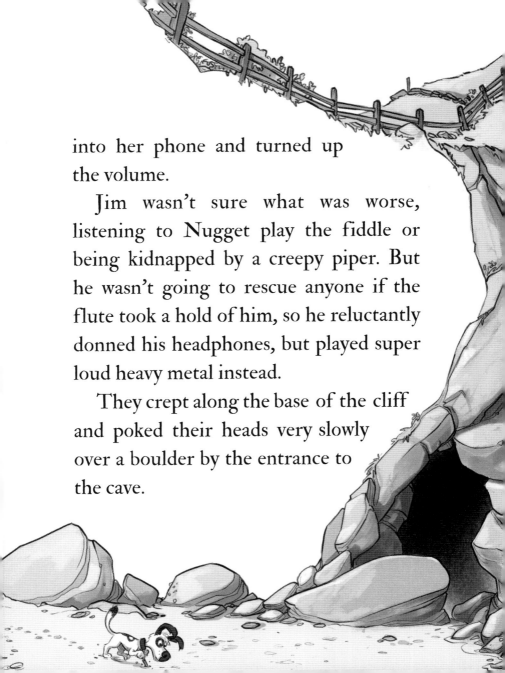

into her phone and turned up
the volume.

Jim wasn't sure what was worse,
listening to Nugget play the fiddle or
being kidnapped by a creepy piper. But
he wasn't going to rescue anyone if the
flute took a hold of him, so he reluctantly
donned his headphones, but played super
loud heavy metal instead.

They crept along the base of the cliff
and poked their heads very slowly
over a boulder by the entrance to
the cave.

From deep inside, soaring through the gloom and shadows, came the sound of a flute. Luckily, neither Jim nor Matilda could hear it. They peered inside, their eyes adjusting to the dim light, to see the Pirate Piper perched on a rock in the centre of the cave, playing his flute.

He was surrounded by hundreds of Dull-on-Sea's children, completely bewitched by the music.

# 11.
# A Theory

Jim and Matilda retreated across the sand, back to the steps by the cliff face. Bones was reluctant to leave the children in the cave so sat guard, behind the boulder and out of view of the Piper.

"We need a plan!" said Jim, pulling his headphones from his ears and resting

them round his neck. "That cursed Piper has them kids under his spell and we've gotta rescue them!"

"I've been thinking about that," said Matilda. "And I've developed a theory."

Jim wasn't entirely sure what a 'theory' was.

"What if Nugget's fiddle music is more powerful than the Pirate Piper's flute?" Matilda started.

"What if Nugget could enchant those children? And take them home?"

"More like drive them away!" scoffed Jim. "Nugget's never enchanted me!"

"But don't you think it's funny that the only child in town who wasn't drawn to the Pirate Piper's flute was ME? And I just happened to be listening to Nugget's music when the Piper took the children?

"And the moment I heard Nugget on the beach the other day, I had to run and listen. I couldn't stop myself. And there were other children too, almost every child on the beach. I've got a plan and we need Nugget and her fiddle," said Matilda.

"Don't like the sound of any plan involvin' that cursed fiddle," said Jim, dreading the thought of listening to

Nugget play. "But I could borrow yer bike and fetch her."

"You stay here and guard the cave with Bones. I'm probably faster than a pirate on a bike anyway," said Matilda. "I'll collect Nugget, but I need to pop in to see my dad on the way."

Matilda peddled as fast as she could to Dull-on-Sea, dropping by her dad's office on her way to the harbour. She scribbled some instructions on a few sheets of paper and explained the plan to him. When she was sure he understood it all, and that the plan was top, top secret, she jumped back on her bike. Her dad waved her off.

"If Mum calls, tell her I'm fine and I'm

playing on the beach with Jim Lad and Bones!" she said as she set off down the street. "And I'll see her at tea time!"

When Matilda arrived at the Jolley-Rogers' ship, she saw a police car by the gangplank and her mum with two police constables talking to Jim's dad. She hid her bike behind an old fishing boat that was raised up on planks, waiting to have its hull repainted.

Matilda watched her mum closely,

knowing that if she revealed herself there was no way she'd be allowed to return to Contraband Cove.

She could talk to the police perhaps, but Chief Inspector Klewless was renowned for messing things up. Also, most of the constables loved playing with their blue lights and sirens, so the Pirate Piper would hear them coming. Matilda was pretty sure that her plan would the best way to return the children to Dull-on-Sea, safe and sound.

And then she spotted Nugget, practising her fiddle on the *Blackhole's* poop deck. Matilda crept along the quayside, darting between coils of ropes,

lobster pots and barrels. Soon she was at the ship's stern, beneath the poop deck, hiding behind a bin. She waited for a gap in the music, grabbing her opportunity when Nugget paused to pick her nose.

"Nugget! Psssst!" Matilda hissed. "Down here!"

Nugget peered over the rail of the ship and waved. "Hi, Matilda!"

"Shhhhh!" said Matilda urgently. "We've got to be quiet! I need you to come with me!"

"But Dad said I had to stay 'ere, cause he reckons that bilge rat, the Pirate Piper, has kidnapped all them kids," said Nugget, pointing to the Piper's ship. "And I don't wanna be kidnapped, at least not until I be finishin' me fiddle practice."

"That's just it," said Matilda. "I want you to come and practise with me, because I LOVE your fiddle playing! Me and Jim will keep you safe. If everything goes to plan, you'll be practising in front of your biggest audience EVER!

A big secret concert, with all the kids of Dull-on-Sea!"

"Really?" said Nugget. "A concert?"

"Really! The biggest, most SECRET concert!" Matilda answered. "Look! There's a rope you can shimmy down..."

Moments later, they were hurtling out of town, Matilda pedalling as fast as her legs would turn the pedals, and Nugget giggling behind her with the wind in her hair and her fiddle case under one arm.

Waiting on the beach, Jim was relieved to see Matilda skipping down the steps, and almost as relieved to see Nugget close behind with her fiddle.

"Ye were aaaages!" said Jim. "I was worryin' ye'd got lost or been kept indoors by the grown-ups!"

"Mum was at the *Blackhole*," Matilda said. "With the police... Talking to your dad. We need to get cracking before they notice Nugget is missing too. We don't want them mucking up our plan!"

# 12.
# BAIT

"I want the Pirate Piper to think you've escaped," explained Matilda, holding Jim by his shoulders. "You walk past the cave entrance and wait until he spots you. Don't go too close. The tide's quite far out, so that should give you some space and a good head start. When you see the Piper come after you, head for the dunes and wait for Bones!"

"Okay," said Jim. "Got it, cap'n!"

Jim Lad staggered across the sand, weaving left and right, like one of those zombies he'd seen on TV. He made groaning noises and was putting on his best blank facial expression. Jim reckoned he was a master at improvising, and if he hadn't been born a pirate, scourge of the seven seas, he would have quite liked to be a famous actor.

Matilda was briefing Nugget, who had already removed her fiddle from its case. Her bow was poised and she was desperate to start playing.

"You have to wait," said Matilda, sternly. "You have to wait until I tell you to play! Jim has to draw the Pirate Piper from the cave first. When Jim's taken the Piper far enough away, you can start."

"Oh, right. I'm glad that Jim and that Piper fella won't be listenin'," said Nugget, suddenly content to wait a while. "I don't think Jim's that keen on my fiddle playin', and that Piper looks to be one of those miserable sorts who don't appreciate the musical talents of children."

Matilda pointed Jim's telescope at the cave, desperate for the Piper to leave. Bones was still sitting behind the boulder, guarding the entrance. Matilda saw him suddenly crouch down, tail wagging, tummy on the ground and his jaw flat to the sand. A tattered figure ran from the cave, looking towards Jim who was zig-zagging across the beach in the distance.

The Pirate Piper played his flute, but Jim didn't turn. Jim was listening to heavy metal music on a volume setting that his parents definitely wouldn't approve of, but at least he knew it would drown out the Piper's flute and Nugget's fiddle. The Pirate Piper ran after him, still frantically blowing into his flute.

"Ready?" Matilda asked Nugget.

"Let's go!"

Matilda and Nugget ran to the cave entrance, crouched over and hugging the edge of the cliff, just in case the Pirate Piper returned. But he didn't, and soon Matilda and Nugget were peering into the darkness at hundreds of dazed children, still under the Pirate Piper's spell.

"Raise that fiddle, Nugget!" said Matilda. "It's concert time!"

Nugget climbed onto the boulder at the entrance to the cave, propped the fiddle beneath her chin and dragged the bow across the strings.

SCREEEEEECH!

All the children turned to Nugget.

They started ambling towards her, like a happy, swaying zombie crowd. While Nugget's fiddle bewitched the children, Matilda gave Bones his orders and a crunchy dog biscuit. He sat wagging his tail, head cocked to one side, listening intently. "You stay right here until I whistle, got it?" she said.

"Woof!" said Bones.

"Righto, Nugget, follow me and keep

playing!" said Matilda and they headed back to the rickety steps by the cliff face, with a swaying mass of children trudging across the sand behind them.

At the top of the steps, with all the children surrounding Nugget on the footpath,

Matilda stuck her fingers between her lips and whistled as loudly as she could. Bones' ears pricked up. He had been waiting patiently for Matilda's signal and soon he was just a bouncy speck in the distance, chasing after Jim and the Pirate Piper.

Jim kept walking, still trying to look like he lacked control, but heading with more purpose into the dunes. The Pirate Piper was gaining on him. Jim hoped everything had gone to plan at the cave, and that Nugget's fiddle had had the desired effect, but he couldn't make a run for it until he'd got the signal. He needed to know that

Matilda and Nugget and the children of Dull-on-Sea were well on their way.

"WOOF!" said Bones, bounding through the grass that sprouted from the undulating dunes. But Jim couldn't hear him above the booming heavy metal in his headphones. Bones grabbed Jim's stripy sash and pulled him behind a crooked, windswept tree. The Pirate Piper, stumbling along the bumpy dunes and glancing at the ground so he wouldn't trip, had taken his eye off Jim at just the right time.

"Bones! You did it! Are they safe?" asked Jim, hugging his wooden-legged dog, who woofed in response. "Great! Let's get out of 'ere!"

The Pirate Piper scowled and almost broke his flute, whacking it against a spindly fence. He had lost sight of Jim and couldn't understand how any child had escaped his magic. He stomped back to the cave, muttering under his breath and wondering if he should move the children, just in case that pesky boy gave away their location.

The Pirate Piper still had his head down, lost in a fog of curses, when he entered the cave. He lifted his chin and raised the flute to his lips, but as he opened his eyes, they widened in horror.

The cave was empty.

# 13.
# Fury!

Captain Horatio Rattus kicked open the doors to the Town Hall. Rats swarmed around him, running between the benches and across people's feet. He had stormed back to town in a haze of fury and gone straight to his ship to release the rats. They had followed the furious flute, from the quayside to the Town Hall, in a blur of fur and frantic squealing.

"Where is that CURSED boy?" he

yelled, purple blood pumping through the veins on his forehead.

"Where are my childrrren?"

The children were all there, in the Town Hall, where they had been led by Nugget.

An hour earlier, Matilda had cycled slowly into town, with Nugget standing across her back wheel playing her fiddle. Behind them was a great swaying mass of children.

Matilda had phoned the mayor and told him to gather the worried parents. She had cycled right into the Town Hall, with Nugget's music leading the children all the way into their sobbing parents' arms. Matilda's mum had hugged her so tight she thought she was about to burst.

But now, with the Pirate Piper's appearance, the children were really clinging to their parents. Or were their parents clinging to them? It was hard to tell, but there was a lot of clinging going on. And there were a LOT of rats.

"You have 'em now," grumbled the Piper, scanning the room and peering into their frightened eyes. "But hold 'em close, squeeze 'em tight, don't let 'em sleep. I can take 'em again, whenever I choose..."

"Well, I'm glad we didn't pay! You are a con man, sir!" said the mayor, unaware of the rat that was munching on his ceremonial hat. "You brought the rats to

Dull-on-Sea! And then you had the nerve
to ask for money to take them away!"

"Ye'll wish you had paid!" smirked the
Piper. "Ye'll be wantin' to pay me, and pay
me tonight! Twenty thousand pounds.
By sunrise. Delivered to my ship.
Or ye'll all be payin' a FAR
heavier price!"

"A far heavier price...?"

enquired the mayor, noticeably rattled. "You don't scare me!"

"I'll be takin' them ALL. Away to sea. Beyond the reach of yer pirate girl's magic." The Piper eyed Nugget and her fiddle suspiciously. He played a couple of bars on his flute, and parents gasped as their children tried to pull away towards him, eyes rolling back in their heads. "And I'll be leavin' these RATS 'ere for good!"

"Twenty thousand pounds," the Piper added. "That's only a few hundred pounds per child, by my reckonin'. Surely yer little darlings are worth that..."

And he turned and left, leaving a Town Hall full of rats, confused children, and worried parents.

# 11.
# DEMANDS

Once the Pirate Piper had left the Town Hall, there was silence. Nobody said a word. The mayor, the councillors, the townsfolk and even Mrs Bumble, were wide-eyed, surrounded by rats and unsure of what to do, or say, next.

"Excuse me, Cap'n Carrot..." said Jim Lad, raising his hand at the back of the room. All eyes turned to Jim, who had

just walked in after a long stroll from Contraband Cove with Bones. "It was my little sister, Nugget, that returned yer kids, with the help of Matilda'n'all. We reckon we could help you out with Cap'n Rattus and them rats, and we won't go chargin' twenty thousand pounds neither."

Mayor Harvey Carrot grumbled under his breath with a grimace he tried to hide in his bejewelled fingers. The last thing he needed was children, especially pirate children, coming up with daft plans. He coughed, putting on his best smile.

"Oh, how lovely. That's splendid. So how would you clever kiddiwinks propose to save the day?"

"I can play a magic fiddle!" chirped Nugget, proudly. "I can get rid of the rats and save the children!"

"A magic fiddle, eh? And what would your fee be, young lady?"

"As much ice cream and candyfloss as I can eat!" said Nugget. "Every time I visit Dull-on-Sea!"

"Done!" said the mayor with a smug grin. At least this might keep the gullible townsfolk happy while he came up with a proper plan.

"Nugget can eat a LOT of ice cream," Jim whispered, giggling with Matilda. "They might've been better payin' the Piper."

"And a statue!" Nugget added. "I'd be likin' a statue!"

"A statue...?" the mayor looked puzzled.

"Aye!" chirped Nugget with a wide grin. "A statue of ME! On the quayside, with my fiddle 'n' all!"

"Of course," the mayor agreed, his fingers crossed behind his back. "You shall have a fine statue, on the harbourside, and it shall be bedecked in flowers every year to celebrate your triumph!"

Everyone cheered, and Nugget looked particularly happy. She couldn't wait to have her own statue.

The mayor couldn't wait to get back to his office.

# 15.
# HI-FI

Mayor Harvey Carrot didn't realise how sophisticated Matilda's plan was.

It had enlisted the help of Norbert Grimes and Matilda's dad, experts in rat catching and hi-fi respectively. Matilda had given her dad some very detailed instructions when she called by his office earlier that day. She knew that the Pirate Piper's ship would lie empty in the harbour while he held the children in the cave and chased Jim Lad around the dunes, and this was crucial to her plan. She had asked her dad to call Norbert Grimes, but to tell nobody else of the plan, and most definitely, definitely, definitely, not to tell Mum.

An hour or so earlier, while the Pirate Piper was still playing his flute to the children in the cave, Matilda's dad parked his car on the quayside. He was wearing black gloves, black trainers, black socks, black jeans, black underpants and a black polo-neck his wife had given him as a Christmas present three years earlier.

He'd never worn it because it was a bit

clingy, especially around his tummy, but he had seen plenty of spy movies and he knew that espionage and sneaking about called for appropriate clothing, even if it did make him feel a bit self-conscious.

It was also the first time he'd worn the black leather gloves his mother-in-law had bought him for his fortieth birthday.

"Evening!" said Arthur Poppycock, arriving for his shift. "New jumper? What are you doing here?"

Matilda had mentioned this in her plan, and her dad was expecting Arthur to arrive.

"Oh, I just fancied a bit of fishing," he said. "By the way, have you heard that chocolate brownies are on special offer at

Super-Duper-Market? Buy one, get one free apparently. And their finest spiced rum is half-price too. You'd better be quick, they shut soon."

"Oh, that is interesting," said Arthur. He dropped his bag in the harbour office and rushed up the street. "Keep an eye on the harbour, could you please? I'll be back in half an hour!"

Matilda's dad was very impressed with his daughter's attention to detail.

He unloaded his car, pushed his wheelbarrow up the rearmost gangplank of the Pirate Piper's ship and set about the work Matilda had asked him to do.

A few minutes later, Norbert Grimes joined him below deck, glancing nervously at his watch.

"Looks like you know what you're doing," he squeaked, admiring the coils of wire and brass plugs that Matilda's dad was connecting so adeptly. "I'd better get to work sharpish."

By the time Arthur Poppycock arrived back at the harbour office, laden with two bulging Super-Duper-Market carrier bags, Matilda's dad was relaxing on the quayside, waiting for a nibble on his fishing line. A short while later, he saw the Pirate Piper appear, marching across the quayside in a rage. The Piper boarded the *Black Death* and reappeared moments later, flute pressed to his lips and followed by a plague of rats, which was just what

Matilda had said would happen.

Meanwhile, Norbert was trundling down the promenade in his clapped-out work van, hoping he would get one over on Captain Horatio Rattus and restore the Grimes' family's good rat-catching name.

# 16.
# NUGGET'S
# BEAUTIFUL MUSIC

Nugget felt surprisingly awake considering it was two o'clock in the morning. She eagerly lifted the fiddle to her chin. Even though she was a pirate, her parents rarely let her stay up this late, and her fiddle playing was definitely not encouraged by anyone but Grandpa. She would have a new audience tonight and was very excited. Nugget drew her bow across the strings...

"SCREEEEEEEEECH!" sang her fiddle, searing through the darkness. All the rats in Dull-on-Sea stopped what they were doing, sat up on their haunches, noses and whiskers twitching, and sniffed the night air.

Nugget's dad was with her, clutching a tourist guide to Dull-on-Sea, complete

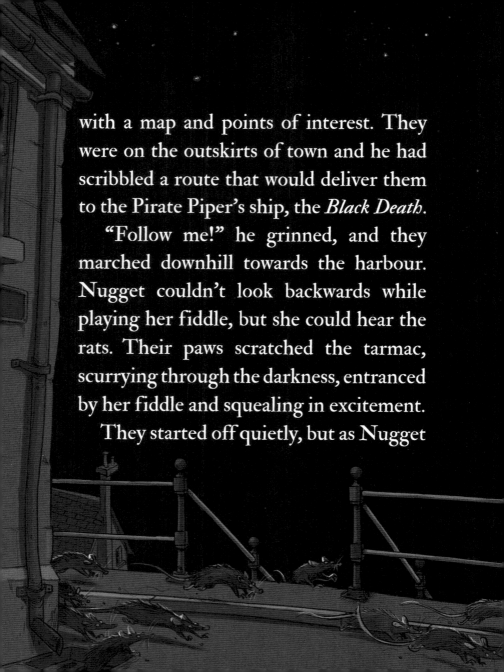

with a map and points of interest. They were on the outskirts of town and he had scribbled a route that would deliver them to the Pirate Piper's ship, the *Black Death*.

"Follow me!" he grinned, and they marched downhill towards the harbour. Nugget couldn't look backwards while playing her fiddle, but she could hear the rats. Their paws scratched the tarmac, scurrying through the darkness, entranced by her fiddle and squealing in excitement.

They started off quietly, but as Nugget

followed her dad through town, the rats
became louder and louder, a riotous din
that almost drowned out her music.

Nugget came to a halt beside the *Black
Death*. She hopped onto a bollard, wearily
playing her fiddle to an audience of ten
thousand rats. She raised her bow
from the strings
and stopped.

"MUSIC!" Matilda hollered into her walkie-talkie, watching from her vantage point in the harbour office.

Arthur Poppycock was fast asleep beside her and oblivious to the night's events.

Matilda's dad, now parked on Sea View Terrace wearing his spy gear and a head-torch, pressed 'play' on his control box. In an instant the harbour was filled with Nugget's music, no longer from the strings of her fiddle, but from an array of tiny, powerful speakers installed around Captain Horatio Rattus's cabin.

The Pirate Piper sat up straight in his bunk and whacked his head on a beam. Fiddle music screeched in his ears.

"What's that 'orrible noise?" he cursed, his eyes scouring the cabin for its source.

"It sounds like a kraken pullin' the gizzards from a mermaid!"

He fell from his bed, hands over

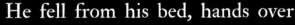

his ears, before extending one hand to search for a door handle in the dim light. Fumbling in the darkness, he grabbed the brass knob and began to turn. Beyond the thick, wooden door, hewn from a single piece of oak, carved with rat motifs and scarred by the patina of hundreds of years of clawing rats, he could hear a rumbling noise.

It was coming from beyond his cabin, intensifying into a crescendo of pounding feet, with a rhythm tied to the fiddle music that filled his head.

The Pirate Piper opened the door and was instantly swamped by rats.

Thousands of them piled on top of him, knocking him off his feet, as they swarmed frantically in search of the fiddle. He struggled to breathe, fur covering his mouth while tiny claws scratched into his face and hands. He tried to get up but it was no good, the rats kept coming, filling his cabin from floor to ceiling, pinning him to the floor.

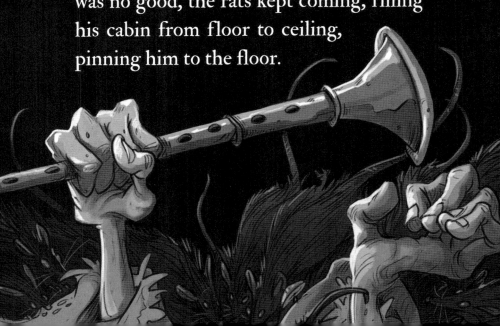

Norbert Grimes was parked across the harbour in his van. He peered through the steamed up windscreen, his thumb trembling over a detonator switch in his right hand.

"BOOM!" Matilda shouted into her walkie-talkie as the last of the rats scurried aboard the Piper's ship.

On cue, Norbert pressed the detonator, and a series of tiny explosions lit up the edge of the *Black Death's* poop deck. Huge nets flew outwards, enveloping the rats, giving them nowhere to go but Captain Horatio Rattus's cabin.

At that very moment, Jim's dad swung an axe down on the last remaining rope that tethered the *Black Death* to the quay. The ship groaned with its release, old timbers creaking as they readjusted themselves and settled, heavy on the water. Trapped in his cabin, beneath thousands of squirming rats, the Pirate Piper heard an engine spluttering into life beyond the ship's bow.

Jim's Grandpa twisted the ignition key of their amphibious truck. It churned the harbour water with its propeller, as sturdy shackles took up the strain on a thick rope that bound it to the *Black Death*, dragging her slowly towards the open sea.

Jim and his mum were aloft, dropping the *Black Death's* tattered sails and tying fast the yards, angled perfectly to take the wind. When they were done, they slid down the tow line and into the amphibious truck. Jim settled in the front seat, next to Grandpa, while his mum released the towing shackles on the truck's stern. They turned to starboard, out of the ship's path, before Grandpa eased off the throttle and they watched the *Black Death* pass, muffled screams and squeals escaping from the ornate windows of the captain's cabin. The *Black Death's* course had already been set, plotted

on the Pirate Piper's own sea charts by torchlight, an hour or two earlier while he snored in his cabin below. The wheel had been tied fast with heavy rope. Jim's dad had done his best to ensure that this would be a one-way voyage, far across the ocean on the whim of the wind and tides.

# 17.
# SUNRISE

Jim and Matilda sat on the harbour wall, legs dangling over the edge and taking turns to look through Jim's telescope. In the distance they could just make out the masts of Captain Horatio Rattus's ship disappearing over the horizon into the golden glow of the early morning sun.

"How long do you think it'll take him to get out of his cabin?" Matilda asked.

"Arrr, I don't rightly know," said Jim. "It'll be tricky f'sure. But even if he does, I doubt he'll be returnin' to Dull-on-Sea."

"You know, I asked my dad to hide the sound system deep beneath the fo'c's'le, right at the front of the ship," said Matilda. "It'll be streaming Nugget's fiddle, playing on an endless loop to the speakers at the stern. I figured that the rats could gnaw through the nets if they really wanted to, but only if the music stopped and the fiddle's spell was broken."

"Aye, he could be there a while then!" Jim chuckled. "Shall we go 'n' join the party?"

It was still early, but in the town square celebrations were in full swing. The people of Dull-on-Sea had woken to a town that was empty of rats, while their children were still safe in their beds. Many people hadn't slept at all. Every parent in Dull-on-Sea had stuffed their children's ears with cotton wool or earplugs, locked their doors and spent the whole night standing guard, just in case.

Jim and Matilda weaved through the crowds, making their way to a stage that overlooked the harbour. On the stage, Matilda's dad was being presented with a voucher to spend at Dull Stereo Systems – to replace the expensive equipment he'd installed on the Pirate Piper's ship – and a key to Dull-on-Sea. He wasn't entirely sure what that meant but it was a very large key. He was more concerned with how his tummy would look on the front page of the *Dull Times,* because he hadn't had time to change out of his espionage outfit.

Jim's dad was presented with a golden axe, after his impressive rope chopping, and Jim's mum was given a voucher for Big Bob's Block and Tackle shop, so she could update her rigging.

Norbert Grimes was given a promotion and was now Chief Rat Catching Consultant for Dull-on-Sea Council. He had a new office, under the

stairs, and a shiny plaque with his name on it. He would also receive a small pay rise and a flashing light and sirens for his van roof.

Jim and Matilda, who had been politely clapping from the front row, were called on stage. Mayor Carrot presented each of them with a stick of Dull-On-Sea rock, an enormous golden medal and unlimited entry to Dull Funfair. But the mayor had been saving the best for last. He called Nugget, who had refused to let go of her fiddle, to the front of the stage.

"And here is NUGGET, the HERO of the hour!" he boomed, to loud applause and cheers from the crowd.

Nugget went bright red, but managed a wave and a bow to the crowd.

She hoisted the fiddle to her chin, ready to play her biggest concert yet, but the mayor asked her to wait a moment for one more announcement.

"Ladies and gentleman, children, pirates and rogues... As Mayor of Dull-on-Sea I do decree that this day, the twenty-second of July, shall henceforth be called NUGGET DAY!" Harvey Carrot hoped that his generosity and a happy ending would secure his re-election. "Every year, on this day, we shall have a parade along the promenade and sing sea shanties!"

"What about my ice creams and

candyfloss?" Nugget asked.

"Oh, yes, of course!" grumbled Harvey Carrot into the microphone, forcing a smile for the *Dull Times* photographer.

The crowd cheered again.

"And don't forget my statue! I want my statue on the quay the next time I visit, or I'll be bringin' them rats back!" added Nugget, readying the bow above her strings as the mayor struggled to maintain his smile.

"Get ready to dance, yer scurvy lubbers!"

Nugget let rip with her fiddle.

The End

# Don't miss Jim Lad and Matilda's other swashbuckling adventures.

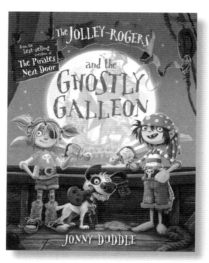

ISBN: 978-1-84877-240-3

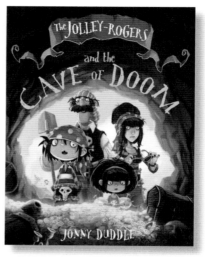

ISBN: 978-1-84877-241-0

ISBN: 978-1-78370-445-3